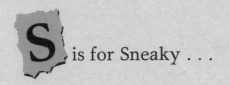

**S** is for Sneaky . . .

Josh flipped up the latch on his locker door. His jacket hung on the hook. His books were stacked on the shelf. His brown-bag lunch was perched on the books.

But in front of the lunch bag was a twisted piece of white paper.

"What's *that*?" Josh asked. "I didn't put that there."

When Josh untwisted the paper, a metal object fell onto the floor.

But Dink, Josh, Ruth Rose, and their teacher were all staring at the paper in Josh's hand.

It was a drawing of a smiling skeleton.

*This book is dedicated to Andrew Stern.*
*—R.R.*

*To Todd, and the skeleton at Marlborough College*
*—J.S.G.*

Text copyright © 2003 by Ron Roy
Cover art copyright © 2015 by Stephen Gilpin
Interior illustrations copyright © 2003 by John Steven Gurney

All rights reserved. Published in the United States by Random House Children's Books, a division of Random House LLC, a Penguin Random House Company, New York. Originally published in paperback by Random House Children's Books, New York, in 2003.

Random House and the colophon and A to Z Mysteries are registered trademarks and A Stepping Stone Book and the colophon and the A to Z Mysteries colophon are trademarks of Random House LLC.

Visit us on the Web!
SteppingStonesBooks.com
randomhousekids.com

Educators and librarians, for a variety of teaching tools, visit us at RHTeachersLibrarians.com

*Library of Congress Cataloging-in-Publication Data*
Roy, Ron.
The school skeleton / by Ron Roy ; illustrated by John Steven Gurney.
p. cm. — (A to Z mysteries)
"A Stepping Stone book."
Summary: At Green Lawn Elementary, the entire school becomes involved in a mystery when Mr. Bones, the skeleton in the nurse's office, disappears.
ISBN 978-0-375-81368-9 (trade) — ISBN 978-0-375-91368-6 (lib. bdg.) —
ISBN 978-0-307-54543-5 (ebook)
[1. Skeleton—Fiction. 2. Lost and found possessions—Fiction. 3. Schools—Fiction. 4. April Fools' Day—Fiction. 5. Mystery and detective stories.] I. Gurney, John, ill. II. Title. III. Series: Roy, Ron. A to Z mysteries.
PZ7.R8139 Sc 2003 [Fic]—dc21 2002008918

Printed in the United States of America
33 32

This book has been officially leveled by using the F&P Text Level Gradient™ Leveling System.

# A to Z Mysteries®

# The School Skeleton

COME HOME, MR. BONES

WE MISS YOU!

by **Ron Roy**

illustrated by
**John Steven Gurney**

A STEPPING STONE BOOK™

Random House ⌂ New York

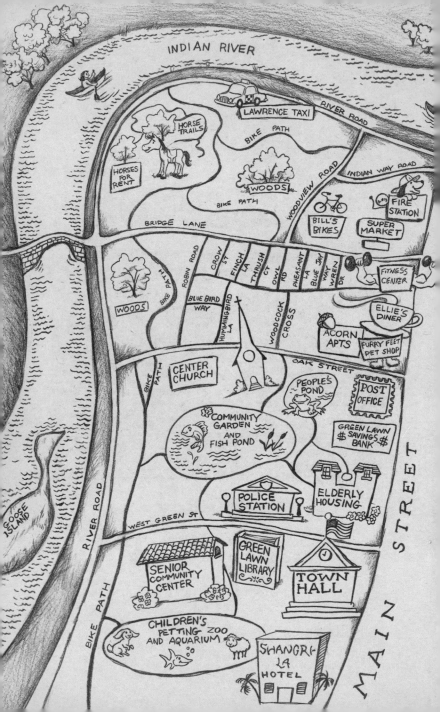

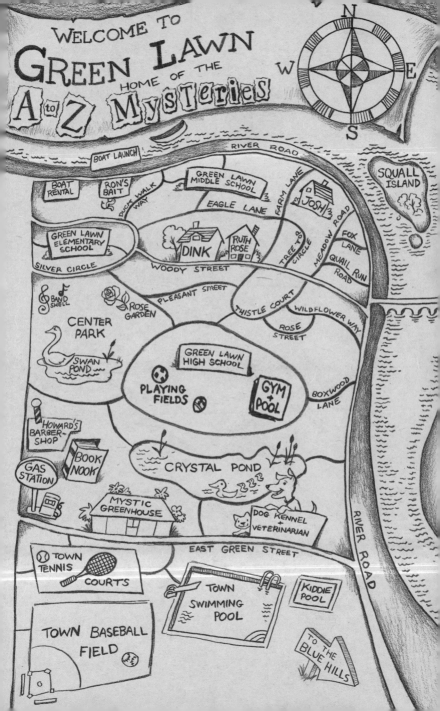

# CHAPTER 1

"Dink, would you mind passing out math paper to everyone?" Mrs. Eagle asked.

"Oh, no, a math quiz," Josh groaned.

Mrs. Eagle smiled. "Yes, Josh. We have one every Monday at ten o'clock," she said. "Now, I'd like to see bright eyes, quick minds, and sharp pencils!"

Kids fumbled inside their desks for pencils. Then some of them formed a line at the pencil sharpener.

Dink liked his teacher and his room.

Everywhere he looked he saw books, cheerful posters on the walls, and sunlight coming through the windows. Mrs. Eagle had brought in a rug and some big pillows for the reading corner. That was Dink's favorite spot in the room.

Dink's full name was Donald David Duncan. But when he first learned to talk, all he could say was "Dink!" Now that was his permanent nickname.

He walked to the paper shelf, grabbed a stack, and began handing it out to the other third graders.

When Dink got to his friend Josh's desk, Josh grinned and whispered,

*Teacher's pet, teacher's pet.*
*When Dink gets sick,*
*he goes to the vet.*

Josh Pinto was tall and thin. He had red hair that liked to fall over his freckled forehead.

Dink crossed his eyes at Josh. Then he slid a piece of paper onto his desk.

"Can I have two?" Josh asked, pulling another sheet from Dink's stack.

"Ouch!" Dink yelped, looking at his finger. There was a thin cut, and it was beginning to bleed.

"What's the matter?" Mrs. Eagle asked, walking over to Dink.

"I got a paper cut," Dink said.

"I'll bet that hurts," Mrs. Eagle said, handing him a tissue. "You'd better go to the nurse's office and get a Band-Aid."

Dink pressed the tissue against his cut and headed for the door. When he passed Ruth Rose's desk, she grinned at him. "Hurry back for the quiz!" she teased.

Ruth Rose Hathaway lived next door to Dink on Woody Street. She had bouncy black hair and quick blue eyes. She always dressed in one color, from head to toe. Today's color was daffodil yellow.

"I'll be back," Dink said. He left the room and headed toward the nurse's office. Mr. Neater, the tall, white-haired school janitor, was sweeping the floor. He wore a metal key ring on his belt. The keys jangled when he pushed the broom. He waved at Dink.

Dink showed him his cut.

"Ooh, bet that hurts," Mr. Neater said.

Dink walked past a long line of lockers and bulletin boards. His paper cut was stinging, so he squeezed the tissue tighter.

When he passed the principal's office, the secretary, Mrs. Waters, was sitting at her desk. Behind her, through another door, Dink saw the principal,

Mr. Dillon, talking on the telephone.

Mrs. Waters smiled at Dink. "Are you here to see Mr. Dillon?" she asked.

Dink stopped at the doorway and held up his finger. "Paper cut," he said.

Mrs. Waters shook her head. "Bet that hurts," she said.

Dink nodded and hurried next door to the nurse's office. Miss Shotsky was staring at her calendar when Dink walked in.

"Can you believe it's almost the end of March?" she asked Dink. "Eighty-two days till summer vacation!"

Dink held up his finger. "Um, I got a paper cut," he said.

"Ooh, I'll bet that hurts," Miss Shotsky said. "I'll have to amputate." Dink's mouth fell open, and Miss Shotsky burst out laughing. Then Dink laughed, too.

"Come on in the back, where I keep

all my torture stuff," the nurse said. She led Dink through a doorway behind her desk.

Miss Shotsky pointed to the examining table in the middle of the room. "Hop up there, please," she said as she walked over to a white cabinet.

Dink sat on the table and looked around the room. Something smelled nice. Then he noticed a vase of flowers on a table next to a closed door.

Over her shoulder Miss Shotsky said, "I have Batman Band-Aids, Wonder Woman Band-Aids, and bunny rabbit Band-Aids. Your choice, kiddo."

"Batman, please," Dink said. He stared at the corner of the room where the school skeleton usually hung from a hook.

"Miss Shotsky, where's Mr. Bones?"

The nurse had her back to Dink. "Hanging in the corner, where he always is."

Dink stared at the empty corner. The school skeleton had been there as long as Dink could remember. Miss Shotsky would bring it to each classroom when she told the kids how eating vegetables and drinking milk made strong bones. At holiday time, she always dressed Mr. Bones in costumes.

The only thing Dink saw in the corner was a red scarf hanging on a hook. "He's not there," Dink said.

Miss Shotsky turned around. "Don't play tricks on the school nurse," she said, grinning at Dink.

"I'm not," Dink said, pointing at the vacant corner. "Look."

Miss Shotsky looked. Her mouth dropped open. "Well, I'll be hog-tied," she said. "He *is* gone!"

"Maybe someone borrowed him," Dink said.

"I don't know when," she said. "Mr. Bones was right there when I came in at seven-thirty. I know because I put my scarf on him. No, someone swiped my skeleton!"

Miss Shotsky shook her head. "Anyway, let's look at your boo-boo," she said, removing the tissue.

In about five seconds, she had cleaned Dink's finger and wrapped a Batman Band-Aid around it. "Now scoot back to class so I can tell Mr. Dillon about Mr. Bones," Miss Shotsky said. She grabbed Dink's hand and dropped two wrapped chocolates into his palm.

"Thanks a lot," he said.

"You're welcome," she said. "And if you tell anyone the nurse gave you candy, I'll deny it!"

She patted Dink's shoulder and walked him to the hallway. Admiring his Band-Aid, Dink ate one of the chocolates on his way back to class.

Mrs. Eagle had her back to Dink when he walked into his classroom. Every kid's head was bent over the math quiz.

On the way to his seat, Dink dropped the other candy onto Ruth Rose's desk. "Hey, what about me?" Josh squeaked.

Dink grinned and slipped into his seat.

# CHAPTER 2

"Sorry I gave you a paper cut," Josh told Dink at morning recess. The cool March wind made Dink's eyes water. Gray clouds blew across the sky, and a few mounds of snow still hadn't melted.

"No problem," Dink said. A soccer ball rolled against his feet, and Dink kicked it toward a bunch of kids.

"Does it still hurt?" Ruth Rose asked. Her hat and scarf matched the rest of her yellow outfit.

"Nope," Dink said. Then he remembered what had happened in Miss Shotsky's office. "But guess what? Mr. Bones has disappeared!"

"The skeleton?" Josh said.

Dink nodded. "I noticed it was missing when I got my Band-Aid," he said. "Miss Shotsky didn't even know it was gone."

"I wonder if someone stole it," Ruth Rose said. She unwrapped the chocolate Dink had given her.

"Why would anyone steal a skeleton?" Josh said, eyeing the candy in Ruth Rose's hand. "Share?" he asked.

Ruth Rose broke the candy in half and passed a chunk to Josh.

Dink shrugged. "The last time Miss Shotsky saw it was around seven-thirty this morning," he said.

Just then they heard a whistle blow. Everyone lined up and entered the building.

Mrs. Eagle was waiting inside the door. "We're going to the gym for a few minutes," she told her class. "Mr. Dillon has an announcement to make."

Led by their teachers, the third, fourth, and fifth graders trooped into the gym. The kindergarteners and first and second graders were already sitting in rows on the floor. Mr. Dillon was standing under the basketball hoop.

When the bigger kids were also seated, Mr. Dillon smiled. "Good morning, kids!" he said. "I have some sad news to report," he went on. "Earlier today, the school skeleton disappeared out of the nurse's office."

Everyone started to talk. A fifth-grade boy with a deep voice said, "Who'd steal a skeleton? A zombie?" His buddies laughed, and his teacher gave him a look.

"If anyone has any information about the missing skeleton," Mr. Dillon went on, "please raise your hand."

No one raised a hand.

"Well, it seems we have a genuine mystery on our hands," Mr. Dillon said. He smiled at the hundred kids who sat watching him. "And I need your help solving it. So I've decided to offer a reward. The classroom that finds Mr. Bones will get free tickets to the new aquarium in Hartford."

"Ooh!" a lot of kids cried.

Ruth Rose turned to Dink and Josh. "I've been asking my parents to take me," she said.

"Me too," Dink said. "They've got a baby beluga whale!"

"Now you're excused," Mr. Dillon said. "Have a nice day, and best of luck solving the case of the missing skeleton!"

The kids stood up, gathered around their teachers, and left the gym. All around him Dink heard kids talking about the missing school skeleton. He heard one little boy whisper, "Maybe it came alive and walked away!"

"Maybe if we figured out why anyone would want a skeleton," Dink said, "we could figure out who took it."

Dink, Josh, and Ruth Rose thought about this as they followed Mrs. Eagle back to their classroom.

They passed Mr. Neater, cleaning a window. He smiled and waved.

"Maybe *he* took it," Josh whispered. "That key ring probably has keys to all the rooms in the school."

"Josh, why would Mr. Neater want a skeleton?" Ruth Rose asked.

"She's right," Dink said. "You might as well accuse Miss Aria, the music teacher, or Mr. Love, the art teacher."

"Well, someone took it," Josh said.

Ruth Rose was shaking her head. "But why does it have to be an adult?" she asked. "Maybe the fifth graders stole Mr. Bones. Remember when they took that papier-mâché whale from the first-grade room and hung it from the flagpole?"

"Yeah, that was *so* cool," Josh said.

Back in their room, Mrs. Eagle told the kids to take out their writing journals. "Since we have only a little time left before lunch, why don't we spend it writing a story?" she said.

"What about?" Bobby asked.

Mrs. Eagle smiled slyly. "About a vanishing school skeleton!" she said.

# CHAPTER 3

"What did you call your story?" Josh asked Dink at their lockers. It was three o'clock, and everyone was going home.

Dink grinned as he put on his jacket. "It's called 'Josh Stole the School Skeleton and Should Go to Jail Forever,'" Dink said.

"Ha-ha," Josh said.

"Mine's called 'The Skeleton's Curse,'" Ruth Rose said. "Mr. Bones puts a curse on all boys with red hair."

"You guys are a riot," Josh said as the

kids walked toward the exit. Miss Shotsky poked her head out of her office and called to Dink, "How's that finger?"

"Fine, thanks," Dink said, wiggling it at her.

"Well, come on in and let me give you a couple of Band-Aids to take home."

"What a baby," Josh whispered as the three kids piled into Miss Shotsky's office.

"He's just jealous of your Batman Band-Aid," Ruth Rose said.

"Yeah, right," Josh said. "Batman is out. Spider-Man rules the school!"

The kids followed Miss Shotsky into the back room. While Dink got more Band-Aids, Josh and Ruth Rose examined the corner where Mr. Bones usually hung.

"Look, there's a footprint in the dust!" Ruth Rose said.

    Miss Shotsky and Dink walked over to look.

    "It looks like a sneaker," Dink said. "See the zigzag tread?"

"It's the left foot," Josh pointed out.

"An adult's size," Ruth Rose said.

"Maybe the thief made this footprint when he lifted Mr. Bones off the hook," Dink said.

"Could be—it sure isn't *my* footprint," Miss Shotsky said, holding her left foot up. Her white nurse's shoe was shorter, and the tread on the bottom was different.

"Were any teachers in here this morning?" Ruth Rose asked Miss Shotsky.

"Not that I know of," the nurse answered. "After I got here, I went to the teachers' lounge to make coffee. I came back at eight o'clock, but I didn't even look at Mr. Bones."

"So whoever took Mr. Bones had to do it between seven-thirty and eight, right?" asked Josh.

Miss Shotsky shook her head. "Nope. I was in and out of here all morning, visiting the first- and second-grade rooms. Anyone could have taken Mr. Bones any time before ten o'clock, when Dink came in with his paper cut."

Just then there was a soft knock on the examining room door. "Excuse me, but could I sweep this room now?" someone said.

It was Mr. Neater with his broom.

"Hi, Tom, come on in," Miss Shotsky said.

"Could I make a drawing of this footprint before you sweep?" Josh asked Mr. Neater.

"Sure, I'll start in the front office," Mr. Neater said.

"And we should measure it," Ruth Rose said.

Miss Shotsky gave Josh a paper and pencil. She handed Ruth Rose a ruler.

Josh made a quick sketch of the print.

"Be sure to get that zigzag pattern,"

Dink said, peering over Josh's shoulder.

Ruth Rose measured the footprint. "It's exactly eleven inches long," she said. Josh wrote ELEVEN INCHES next to the drawing.

"So all we have to do is find out who wears this kind of shoe," Josh said, "and we find Mr. Bones and win the tickets to the aquarium."

"But a lot of the teachers wear sneakers," Ruth Rose said. "How do we find the right one?"

"I know who we can ask," Dink said. "Mrs. Waters. All the teachers walk past her desk to get their mail. Maybe she notices the shoes they wear."

"Let's hurry before she goes home," Ruth Rose said.

Miss Shotsky opened a small door next to her filing cabinet. "Here's a shortcut to the principal's office," she said.

Sure enough, when the kids walked through the door, there was Mrs. Waters at her desk. She was staring into her open purse.

"Hi, kids," she said, closing her purse and putting it in a drawer. "Still here?"

"We're trying to find the skeleton," Ruth Rose said.

"We found a footprint on the floor where Mr. Bones hangs," Dink said. "It's a sneaker."

"We think the guy who stole the skeleton made the print," Josh said. "If we find him, our room wins the tickets!"

"Just one footprint? Maybe you should be looking for a one-legged thief," Mrs. Waters said with a twinkle in her eye.

Josh giggled and placed his drawing on her desk. "Do you know anyone who wears this kind of sneaker?" he asked.

Just then the small door opened again. Miss Shotsky peeked in, wearing her red scarf.

"Good night, all," Miss Shotsky said. "Happy skeleton hunting, kids."

"Good night, Claire," said Mrs. Waters.

The door closed.

Mrs. Waters studied Josh's drawing, then shook her head. "I usually notice what the teachers are wearing," she said. "But I never see the bottoms of their feet."

She traced the zigzag tread with her finger. "Although this pattern does seem familiar. I feel sure I've seen it somewhere."

She smiled. "Knowing me, I'll think of it halfway home."

Mrs. Waters glanced at the clock and stood up. "Time for me to leave," she said, heading toward her coat closet. But when she tried to open the door, it wouldn't budge.

Mrs. Waters walked back to her desk and pulled her purse and a sweater from a drawer. "First I lose my powder," she said. "Now I think I'm losing my head!"

Just then Mr. Dillon appeared in the doorway to his office. "Hey, kids. Still here?"

Dink told Mr. Dillon about the footprint in Miss Shotsky's examining room. Josh showed him his drawing.

"We think the thief was wearing sneakers like this," Ruth Rose said.

"Well, that leaves me out," Mr. Dillon said. He raised one foot and showed the kids the smooth sole of his shiny tassel loafer.

"Me too," Mrs. Waters said. She pointed a small high-heeled shoe at them. "That footprint is twice as big as my feet!"

# CHAPTER 4

As the kids walked home, Josh studied his drawing of the left footprint. "How can we find the guy who wears this sneaker?" he asked.

"It could be a woman," Ruth Rose said.

Josh turned and grinned. "What about Mrs. Eagle?" he said. "Maybe she stole Mr. Bones."

Ruth Rose laughed. "No, her feet look as small as my mom's," she said. "My mom wears size six."

"Let's go to my house and make a list of all the grown-ups at the school," Dink suggested. "Then we can figure out how to check their shoes."

"Why don't we go to your house and make a snack?" Josh asked. "How about a turkey sandwich and apple pie with vanilla ice cream on top?"

"How about guinea-pig food?" Dink said.

In his kitchen, Dink found a plate of cookies and a note from his mom, saying she was shopping. The kids walked up to Dink's room with the cookies and Josh's drawing.

Dink handed Ruth Rose a pad.

While she wrote, Dink went to his dad's closet and found a pair of his sneakers. On the bottom he found a circle with SIZE TEN stamped inside. Then he got a ruler and measured the sneaker. It was eleven inches long, the same as the footprint they had found in Miss Shotsky's office.

"Guys, I think the skeleton snatcher wears a size ten," he said.

"I'll bet a lot of the male teachers wear that size," Josh said.

Ruth Rose showed them her list. "I got thirteen people," she said.

"Did you count Mr. Dillon and Mr. Neater?" Dink asked.

Ruth Rose nodded. "Yup. All the adults who work at the school."

"We can cross off five names," Josh said. "Mrs. Eagle, Mrs. Waters, and Miss Shotsky all have smaller feet. And Mr. Dillon was wearing loafers today."

"Who's the fifth?" Dink asked.

"The custodian, Mr. Neater," Josh said.

"Why cross him off?" Ruth Rose asked. "He wears sneakers."

Josh laughed. "But they're the biggest sneakers I've ever seen. I think he wears about size thirteen!"

Ruth Rose put an X in front of the names of the five people Josh had mentioned.

Dink looked at the eight remaining names. "Four women and four men," he said, dropping a hunk of cookie into his guinea pig's cage. "Do you think one of them took the skeleton?"

"One way to find out," Josh said. "Check their shoes against my drawing."

"How do we do that?" Dink asked.

"Just tell them about the footprint we found, then ask them if we can measure their feet and check the treads of their sneakers."

"There's one problem," Ruth Rose said. "If one of the teachers did take the skeleton, he won't let us measure his feet!"

"Then we'll know he's the guilty one," Josh said.

"But what if two teachers say no?" Dink asked. "Then we still wouldn't know which one did it."

"But at least we'd have narrowed it down to two," Ruth Rose said. "Then we could figure out what to do next."

"We'd better decide," Josh said. "Every kid at school wants to win those aquarium tickets."

"But we're the only ones who know about the footprint," Ruth Rose said. "We've got a head start."

"Not for long," Josh said. "Miss Shotsky and Mr. Neater saw the footprint, too. And I showed the drawing to Mrs. Waters and Mr. Dillon. Pretty soon the whole school will know."

"Okay, let's talk to those eight teachers tomorrow," Dink said.

"We could put notes in their mailboxes," Ruth Rose suggested.

"Great idea!" Dink said. He sat at his computer, and Josh and Ruth Rose gave him suggestions. This is what they came up with:

DEAR _____,

WE HAVE A CLUE TO THE MYSTERY OF THE MISSING SKELETON. MAY WE TALK TO YOU TODAY? PLEASE CHECK YES \_\_\_\_\_ OR NO \_\_\_\_\_ AND PUT THIS IN MRS. EAGLE'S MAILBOX.

THANK YOU!

SIGNED,

DINK DUNCAN, JOSH PINTO,

AND RUTH ROSE HATHAWAY

Dink printed eight copies. Using Ruth Rose's list of names, the kids addressed a letter to each.

"That should do it," Dink said when they were finished. "We'll ask Mrs. Waters to put them in the mailboxes tomorrow morning."

"And by afternoon, our class will have tickets to the aquarium," Josh said, grinning at his friends.

"Don't get your hopes up yet, Josh," Ruth Rose said.

"Why not? If we find the right shoe, we find the person who took Mr. Bones, right? So we win the tickets, right?"

Ruth Rose shook her head. "Wrong. We have to find the skeleton to win the tickets," she said. "While we're running around measuring people's feet, some other kid might find Mr. Bones!"

# CHAPTER 5

The next morning they met in front of the school before the first bus showed up. There were only a couple of cars in the teachers' parking lot.

"I hope Mrs. Waters isn't late today," Josh said as they entered the school. "We need to get these notes in the mailboxes before the teachers get here."

They hurried along the silent hallway to the principal's office. Mrs. Waters was just taking off her coat.

"Mr. Dillon isn't in yet," she said when the kids walked in.

"We came to see you," Dink said.

"Well, isn't that nice!" the secretary said, flipping a page on her calendar. "Goodness, where did March go already? Now, how can I help you kids?"

Dink, Josh, and Ruth Rose explained their idea.

"You honestly think one of our teachers took that skeleton?" she asked.

"We don't know," Dink said. "But the footprint looks like an adult's. Would you mind putting these in the right mailboxes?"

He handed Mrs. Waters the eight notes they'd printed. She read one and smiled.

"Of course I will," she said. "And I wish you luck finding Mr. Bones. I know Mr. Dillon will be happy to have this mystery solved!"

Mrs. Waters stood up, walked to the teachers' mailboxes, and placed the notes in eight different slots.

The kids thanked her and left. Just then the bell rang, and students began rushing through the front door.

They walked to their room and found Mrs. Eagle at her desk. "My, my, look who's eager to get started!" she said.

Once more, the kids explained about the footprint, the eight notes, and their plan for finding the person who took the school skeleton. They showed her Josh's drawing of the footprint.

"And you plan to ask each teacher if you can measure his or her feet?" Mrs. Eagle asked, grinning.

"That footprint is our only clue," Ruth Rose said.

"We want our class to win the tickets," Josh said.

Mrs. Eagle smiled. "All right, if the

teachers agree, you three may leave the room later," she said.

The morning seemed to last forever. Dink kept glancing at the clock, and Josh kept sighing and fidgeting at his desk.

Finally, during math, a fifth grader came into the room and handed Mrs. Eagle a stack of papers.

She looked through the stack, then called Dink up to her desk. "Here are your responses," she whispered. "All eight have checked YES. You might as well go now, and good luck!"

Dink, Josh, and Ruth Rose quietly left the room. They brought with them eight sheets of drawing paper, a ruler, Josh's footprint sketch, and Ruth Rose's list of teachers' names.

"Guys, I just thought of something," Ruth Rose said in the hallway. "Whoever made that footprint yesterday might be wearing different shoes today."

"You're right," Dink said. "So anyone whose shoe is about the right size, we'll ask if they wore the same shoes yesterday."

They started walking down the hall. On one classroom door, someone had hung a sign. It said: COME HOME, MR. BONES. WE MISS YOU! There was a drawing of a skeleton under the words.

Three girls wearing skeleton masks scampered down the hallway. "Mr. Bones, where are you?" one of the girls said. The other two laughed at their friend.

Outside the fifth-grade room, a paper skeleton hung from the ceiling.

"The whole school is looking for the skeleton," Josh muttered. "We have to find it first!"

"Then we'd better get going," Ruth Rose said. "Maybe no one else knows about the footprint yet."

First on her list was Miss Alubicki,

the kindergarten teacher. They showed her Josh's drawing and asked if she would let them trace her left foot.

"Of course," Miss Alubicki said, smiling. "But I can already tell you, that foot is a lot bigger than mine."

The little kids giggled as Josh traced around her foot on a piece of paper. Outside in the hall, Josh compared it with his drawing.

"It's definitely not her," he said. "Miss Alubicki's foot is only seven inches long."

Ruth Rose drew a big X in front of Miss Alubicki's name on her list. After the name she wrote: TOO SMALL.

They went next door and peeked into Mr. Diodato's first-grade class. The tall teacher was writing at the chalkboard: WHO STOLE THE SCHOOL SKELETON?

Dink knocked, and Mr. Diodato looked up. "We have visitors, class," he said, grinning.

While Josh traced Mr. D.'s sneaker onto a sheet of paper, the first graders gathered around.

Dink, Josh, and Ruth Rose thanked Mr. D. and left. In the hall, Josh measured what he had traced onto the paper. Mr. Diodato's sneaker was almost thirteen inches long. The bottom tread had little squares, not zigzags.

"Cross him off, too," Dink said. Ruth Rose put an *X* by Mr. Diodato's name and wrote: TOO BIG.

"Six more names to go," Josh said, glancing at Ruth Rose's list. "What if it's none of them?"

"It *must* be someone on this list," Dink said. "How could a stranger sneak into the school and walk out with a skeleton?"

One by one, the kids traced teachers' shoes onto paper and measured them. They compared the tracings with Josh's drawing. One by one, Ruth Rose put *X*'s next to the names.

With only one more name to go, Ruth Rose's list looked like this:

✘ KINDERGARTEN—MISS ALUBICKI—TOO SMALL

✘ FIRST GRADE—MR. DIODATO—TOO BIG

✘ SECOND GRADE—MISS CRUMPET—TOO SMALL

✘ THIRD GRADE—MRS. EAGLE—TOO SMALL

✘ FOURTH GRADE—MR. QUATRO—ABSENT
MONDAY

✘ FIFTH GRADE—MRS. GOLDEN—TOO SMALL

✘ PRINCIPAL—MR. DILLON—WAS WEARING
LOAFERS MONDAY

✘ SECRETARY—MRS. WATERS—TOO SMALL

✘ NURSE—MISS SHOTSKY—TOO SMALL

✘ ART TEACHER—MR. LOVE—TOO BIG

✘ MUSIC TEACHER—MISS ARIA—TOO SMALL

✘ JANITOR—MR. NEATER—WAY TOO BIG

GYM TEACHER—MR. PALMER

"Not one of these people could have made that footprint," Ruth Rose said.

"Who's the last name?" Dink asked.

"Mr. Palmer, the gym teacher," she answered.

Josh crossed his fingers. "Maybe he's the one!" he said.

They found Mr. Palmer sitting behind his desk. He smiled when the kids walked into his office.

"I read your note," he said.

"Thanks for seeing us," Dink said. "May we measure your shoes?"

Mr. Palmer grinned. "Sure. But I guarantee I didn't steal that skeleton yesterday morning. I was in the emergency room at the hospital."

He stood up and held out his left foot. There was a white cast on it. "I slipped on some ice getting into my car yesterday," he said.

He pointed to a pair of crutches leaning in a corner. "I can hardly carry my lunch, let alone a skeleton!"

# CHAPTER 6

"I hope your foot gets better fast," Dink said.

"Thanks, and I hope you find the skeleton," Mr. Palmer said.

The kids left and walked toward their room.

"We must've figured something wrong," Josh said. "One of these people has to be the perp."

"The perp?" Dink said.

Josh grinned. "Yeah, you know, the guy that did it."

"So if it wasn't anyone on this list, who was it?" Ruth Rose asked. "That footprint didn't get there by magic."

"I wonder if it could be a trick footprint," Dink said.

"What do you mean?" Josh asked.

"I read a story once about some kids who made fake bear tracks to fool their parents," Dink said. "They taped some rolled-up socks onto an old rake. Then they stamped 'bear' tracks in the snow all around their house."

"But why would the skeleton snatcher leave a fake footprint?" Ruth Rose asked.

Dink shrugged. "Why would anyone steal the school skeleton in the first place?"

"Well, whoever did it is pretty mean," Josh grumbled. "Playing tricks on innocent kids isn't nice!"

Dink and Ruth Rose burst out

laughing. They were still giggling as they got close to their room.

"Wait a sec, I want to put this drawing away," Josh said.

"STOP!" Ruth Rose shouted as Josh stepped up to his locker. "DON'T MOVE!"

"What!" Josh gasped, smacking his chest with one hand. "You almost gave me a heart attack!"

"Look what you almost stepped on!" Ruth Rose pointed to a circle of white powder on the floor. In the center of the circle was a footprint.

It was a very familiar footprint.

Ruth Rose grabbed Josh's footprint sketch from his hand and knelt next to the new print. "Check it out, guys," she said.

Dink and Josh bent down for a closer look. It was a left footprint with a zigzag pattern. When Ruth Rose

placed Josh's drawing on the floor, the
two footprints were identical.

"Oh my gosh!" Josh cried. "The
skeleton snatcher was here!"

Just then Mrs. Eagle popped her
head through the door. "What's going
on?" she asked.

Ruth Rose pointed at the footprint.
"Look, Mrs. Eagle."

"He's back!" Josh said.

"And he came right to your locker," Dink added, grinning. "The zombie is after you!"

"No way!" Josh argued. "See, the footprint is halfway between my locker and yours."

"Maybe he stole something from one of your lockers," Ruth Rose said.

Mrs. Eagle knelt and put her finger in the white stuff. Then she lifted her finger to her nose. "Hmm," she said. "This smells like talcum powder. Why don't you boys open your lockers?"

"You go first," Josh told Dink.

"Okay," Dink said. "Since you're such a scaredy-cat."

"Am not."

"Are too."

"Boys," Mrs. Eagle said.

Dink pulled open his locker door. His jacket hung on a hook. On the shelf, his books were neatly arranged. His lunch bag sat on top of his books.

"Nothing's missing," Dink said. "Now you, Josh."

"No problem," Josh said, flipping up the latch on his locker door. His jacket hung on the hook. His books were stacked on the shelf. His brown-bag lunch was perched on the books.

But in front of the lunch bag was a twisted piece of white paper.

"What's *that*?" Josh asked. "I didn't put that there."

Dink leaned close and whispered, "Maybe it's a note from the snatcher!"

"Yeah, right," Josh said, grabbing the paper twist. "Hey, there's something inside!"

When Josh untwisted the paper, a metal object fell onto the floor.

But Dink, Josh, Ruth Rose, and their teacher were all staring at the paper in Josh's hand.

It was a drawing of a smiling skeleton. Someone had sketched a big "2" in the center of its forehead.

Mrs. Eagle bent down and picked up what had fallen. "How odd," she said, showing the kids a shiny key.

# CHAPTER 7

Dink, Josh, Ruth Rose, and their teacher walked back into the classroom.

"Now we have another mystery to solve," Mrs. Eagle told the class. "Josh, why don't you and Dink and Ruth Rose tell the class what you've been up to?"

The three kids told their classmates about the first footprint and showed them Josh's drawing. Then they explained how they had traced and measured each teacher's shoe to try

and find the one who had left the footprint.

Josh's drawing, Ruth Rose's list, and the eight shoe outlines were on Mrs. Eagle's desk. Also on the desk were the drawing of the skeleton and the key that Josh had found in his locker.

"One more thing," Mrs. Eagle said. "Someone sprinkled powder on the floor near Josh's locker, then made another footprint."

She looked at the class. "Any ideas?"

Bobby raised his hand. "I think the same person who took the skeleton put the key in Josh's locker," he said.

"But why?" asked Ruth Rose. "We don't know what the key goes to."

Mrs. Eagle took the key and walked over to the classroom door. She slipped the key into the keyhole and tried to lock the door.

"It doesn't work in this one," she said. Then she tried the key in her desk lock. "Nor this one."

"We could try all the locks in the school," Frankie suggested.

Mrs. Eagle nodded. "Good idea, Frankie, but there are dozens of doors and desks."

"Could the key go to a suitcase or a safety-deposit box?" Dink asked.

Mrs. Eagle smiled at Dink. "Good thinking."

"Maybe it's the key to someone's house," Tommy said.

"These are all good ideas," Mrs. Eagle said. "But it's not practical to go around Green Lawn trying the key in every keyhole."

"What I can't figure out is why he's doing this," Dink said. "Why leave footprints and a key that he knew we'd find?"

Josh raised his hand. "And why did the guy pick my locker to leave it in?" he asked.

"Maybe he didn't," Ruth Rose said. "The lockers don't have our names on them. The guy might have just picked any third-grade locker."

"You're right," Mrs. Eagle said. "Maybe the key was meant to be found by *anyone* in this room!"

Everyone looked at each other and started whispering.

Mrs. Eagle made a pile of all the evidence on her desk and handed it to Josh along with the key. "But now we have to get back to work," she said.

• • •

It was windier and colder as Dink, Josh, and Ruth Rose walked home after school.

"Let's go to my house," Ruth Rose said. "I'll make hot chocolate."

"With whipped cream?" Josh asked.

"Marshmallows," Ruth Rose said.

"The big, fat ones?"

"No, Josh, the little, bitty ones," Ruth Rose answered.

"I like the big ones," Josh mumbled.

A few minutes later, Ruth Rose let them in with her key. She found a note from her mom, saying she'd taken Ruth Rose's little brother, Nate, to the dentist.

In the kitchen, Ruth Rose's cat, Tiger, was lying on the table in a patch of sun. Ruth Rose shooed Tiger away, then made hot chocolate in the microwave.

Dink and Josh sat at the table. Josh laid the key and the drawing of the skeleton on the sunny spot vacated by Tiger.

"I think we're missing something," Dink said, looking down at the key and the drawing. "The guy steals a skeleton and leaves a footprint. Then he plants a key in your locker and leaves another shoe print in powder that he sprinkled on the floor. He's trying to tell us something, but what?"

Ruth Rose brought three mugs and a bag of marshmallows to the table.

They all floated marshmallows on their hot chocolate.

"I just remembered something," she said. "Didn't Mrs. Waters tell us she was missing her powder?"

"But *she* didn't make that footprint outside my locker," Josh said.

"I know," Ruth Rose said. "But someone could have stolen her powder to use it to make that footprint. Maybe the thief wants everyone to suspect

Mrs. Waters of taking the skeleton."

The kids sipped their hot chocolate and thought about that.

"It would have to be someone who can get into her desk to get the powder," Dink said finally.

"Like Mr. Dillon!" Ruth Rose said.

"Yeah, but the footprints aren't his, either," Josh said. "Remember he was wearing those loafers with no tread on the bottom."

"And why would Mr. Dillon steal something and blame it on his secretary?" Dink asked. "It doesn't make sense!"

"I wonder if anything else has been stolen from the school that we don't know about," Ruth Rose said.

"Well, if anyone would know, it's Mrs. Waters," Dink said. "We could talk to her again tomorrow."

Josh picked up the skeleton picture that had been wrapped around the key.

"What do you guys think this "2" on the skull means?" he asked. "The school doesn't have *two* skeletons, does it?"

"The high school and the middle school might have their own," Ruth Rose said. "Did anyone steal their skeletons?"

"I doubt it, or we'd have heard something," Dink said.

"I don't want to live in a town where some zombie goes around stealing skeletons," Josh grumbled.

"Anyway, this key must mean something," Dink said. He placed the key next to the skull's mouth. "Talk to us, Mr. Bones!"

"Wait a minute!" Ruth Rose cried. She moved the key up a few inches, next to the big "2." "What does that say?"

Josh dropped a marshmallow into his mug. "It says 'key-head,'" he said. "'Key-face'? 'Key-bones'?"

Ruth Rose shook her head. She pointed at the key. "Key," she said. Then she pointed at the number on the skull. "Two," she continued. Then she pointed to the skeleton's body. "Skeleton," she said. "I think it says 'key *to* skeleton'!"

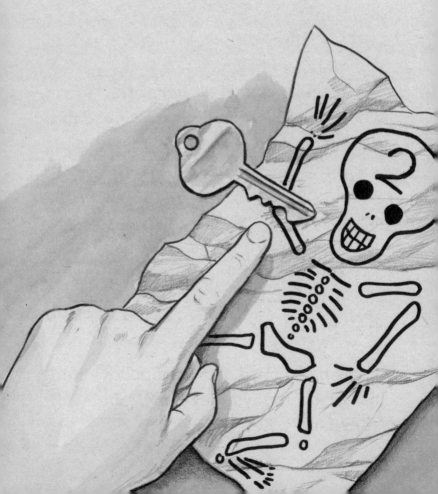

# CHAPTER 8

"I think he's trying to tell us that this key unlocks wherever Mr. Bones is hidden," Ruth Rose continued.

"But where?" Josh asked. "The key could go to a lock in California."

"The skeleton is probably still in the school," Dink said. "How could anyone carry it out of the building in broad daylight?"

"But how could anyone hide it inside the school in broad daylight, either?" Ruth Rose asked. "Somebody would have been bound to notice."

"Unless Miss Shotsky did it," Josh said. "She carries Mr. Bones to classes all the time."

Dink shook his head. "Trust me, she was surprised when she saw the skeleton was missing."

"And that wasn't her footprint," Ruth Rose said.

The kids stared at the drawing and the key.

"Why give us the key?" asked Josh. He had a chocolate mustache. "Does this guy want to get caught?"

"It's almost like he wants us to find Mr. Bones," Ruth Rose said.

"Well, at least no other kid has found the skeleton yet," Dink said. "We can still win aquarium tickets for our class."

Ruth Rose picked up the key and held it close to her eyes. "That's strange. This key looks brand-new," she said.

"How can you tell?" Dink asked.

"There are no scratches on it," Ruth Rose said. "And it's very shiny." She dug her house key out of her pocket. "See, my key has a lot of tiny marks from where it rubs against the inside of the door lock. But Josh's key looks like it was just made."

"So how do we find out what it opens?" Josh asked, slurping the last of his hot chocolate.

"We could ask Mr. Neater," Dink suggested. "He has keys to everything in the building."

"Wait, could he have put the key in Josh's locker?" Ruth Rose asked.

"That would mean he took the skeleton," Dink said. "But his shoes are way too big, remember?"

"Unless he faked the footprints," Josh said, "like those kids who made the bear tracks."

Dink wrapped the key in the skeleton drawing and handed it to Josh. "Let's show him this tomorrow," he said. "And don't lose it. The key is our best clue!"

A few snowflakes fell as Dink, Josh, and Ruth Rose hurried into the school building the next morning.

"Whoever heard of snow on the first of April," Josh muttered. He was wearing a green hat pulled down over his ears.

Mr. Neater had a small office in the school basement. The kids found him there, sitting on a stool in front of a workbench. He was trying to unjam a stapler.

"Good morning, Mr. Neater," Dink said.

The white-haired man turned and smiled. "Hey, kids. What brings you down here? Playing hooky?"

Josh pulled the wrapped key from his pocket. He removed the drawing and showed the key to Mr. Neater. "Have you ever seen a key like this?" he asked.

Mr. Neater held the key under the light over his workbench. He examined both sides before he shook his head. "Nope, don't think so. But I can tell you it's a copy. This key was made from

another, probably in some hardware store."

"You were right!" Josh marveled. "How come you're so smart, Ruth Rose?"

Ruth Rose just smiled.

Mr. Neater unclipped the key ring from his belt and plunked it down on the workbench. He fanned the keys and compared a few with the one Josh had given him. "See, an original key has the name of the company that makes it. Like this one is a Yale key."

He tapped Josh's key. "But yours has no name—it was copied from another key. Where'd you get it?" he asked, handing the key back to Josh.

"It was in my locker with . . ."

Just then a fifth grader came clomping down the basement stairs. He was taller than Dink and had dark brown hair and dark, mischievous eyes.

"Well, hi, Cory," Mr. Neater said. "What's up?"

"I found this in my locker and wondered if you could tell me what it goes to," Cory said. He handed Mr. Neater a shiny key.

Everyone stared at Cory's key.

"Did you find a drawing of a skeleton with the key?" Ruth Rose asked.

Cory nodded. "Yup, all twisted around the key."

"And was there a footprint outside your locker?" Dink asked. "In powder?"

Cory looked suspiciously at Dink. "Yeah. How'd you know?"

"Because there was one near my locker, too," Josh said. "And I found a key in my locker, with this wrapped around it." He showed Cory his picture.

Cory dug into his pocket and drew out a twisted paper. Both boys laid the drawings flat on Mr. Neater's bench. The pictures—like the keys—were identical.

"Say, do you suppose this has anything to do with Miss Shotsky's skeleton disappearing?" Mr. Neater asked.

"Sure it does," Cory said. He pointed to the number "2." "The kids in my class figured it out easy. The key and the picture mean 'key to the skeleton.' We're gonna find the skeleton and get free tickets to the new aquarium!"

More footsteps clunked down the basement stairs. This time it was two second-grade girls. They were holding hands and looked embarrassed to see four older kids there.

"Susan and Jane, right?" Mr. Neater said, smiling at the two little kids.

The girls nodded. Susan nudged

Jane, who opened her hand. "Miss Crumpet wanted to know if you know what this key fits," she said shyly.

The key was the same as the two that Cory and Josh held.

"Bet you found this key in your locker, right?" Mr. Neater said.

Jane nodded. "And a silly picture of a skeleton with a '2' on his head!"

# CHAPTER 9

Green Lawn Elementary didn't have a cafeteria. All the kids brought their lunches from home.

Dink, Josh, and Ruth Rose took their bags outside and sat on the swings in the sun. A lot of other kids came out to eat, too.

"Tuna fish," Josh said, smelling his sandwich. "What've you guys got?"

Ruth Rose peeked inside her plastic bag. "Baloney and cheese," she said.

Dink's sandwich turned out to be

egg salad. "Who wants to trade?" he asked.

"I'll take the egg," Ruth Rose said.

"I want the baloney and cheese," Josh said.

"Good," Dink said. "I wanted the tuna."

The kids swapped sandwiches and began eating.

"A kid from each class in the school found a key and a drawing," Dink said after he'd swallowed his first bite.

"So there are six keys and six drawings and six footprints," Josh said around a mouthful of sandwich.

Ruth Rose shook her head. "Now every class is trying to find Miss Shotsky's skeleton before anyone else does." She sighed. "That's about a hundred kids!"

Two small boys walked past, looking for a place to eat their lunches. One of the boys carried a drawing of a skeleton.

"Even the little kindergartners!" Josh wailed, kicking some sand. "It's not fair."

"I just thought of something," Ruth Rose said. "There's a door that connects Mr. Dillon's office to the nurse's office. He could have snuck in when Miss Shotsky wasn't there and taken the skeleton."

"It would take him only a couple of minutes," Josh said.

"Guys, I thought we already decided the snatcher couldn't be Mr. Dillon," Dink said. "He wasn't wearing sneakers."

"But he could easily have taken Mrs. Waters's powder," Ruth Rose reminded him. "The powder, the door to the nurse's office . . . everything else points to Mr. Dillon."

"But why would the school principal steal the school skeleton?" Dink asked. "He's the one offering the reward for finding Mr. Bones!"

Josh balled up his lunch bag. "Let's go see Mrs. Waters again. Maybe she's remembered where she saw that zigzag sneaker sole."

The kids hurried into the school and headed for the principal's office.

"Let's leave our lunch stuff," Dink said, stopping at his locker. They opened their locker doors and put their lunch bags inside.

They found Mrs. Waters sitting at her desk with a cup of tea in front of her.

She looked up when the kids walked in. "This school has gone wacky," she said. "First Miss Shotsky's skeleton disappears. Then I start losing things. I've been searching for my closet key for two days! Whatever will be next!"

"You're missing a key?" Josh asked, already digging in his pocket.

"Yes. I haven't been able to put my purse and coat in the closet," Mrs. Waters said.

Josh found the skeleton drawing wrapped around the key. He removed the paper and put the key on Mrs. Waters's desk. "Is this it?"

Mrs. Waters picked up the key and examined it. "No, this isn't the one I lost."

"Could it be a copy of your key?" Dink asked.

"I suppose." Mrs. Waters looked at Dink. "Why would anyone take my key and make a copy? Where did you find it, Josh?"

"In my locker," he said. "Along with this." He showed Mrs. Waters the picture of the skeleton.

"A key and a skeleton?" she said. "What does it mean?"

"We think the key leads to the skeleton," Ruth Rose said. "So it might be in your closet!"

"My closet! Who would do such a thing?"

Mrs. Waters stood up and marched over to her coat closet. Dink, Josh, and Ruth Rose followed her.

Mrs. Waters inserted the key into the lock and turned it. The door slowly swung open.

Hanging from Mrs. Waters's coat hook was the school skeleton. Mr. Bones had a big grin on his face.

"IT'S MR. BONES!" Ruth Rose screamed.

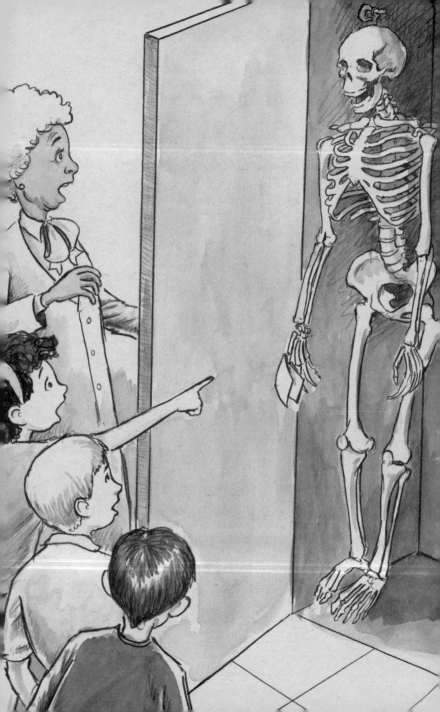

# CHAPTER 10

Mr. Dillon came flying out of his office. "What's the matter?"

Before Mrs. Waters could answer, Miss Shotsky burst into the little room.

"Who screamed? Anyone hurt?" Miss Shotsky cried, looking first at the three kids. "Are you kids all right?"

"Yes, and here's your friend, Miss Shotsky." Mrs. Waters pulled the closet door all the way open.

"Well, for heaven's sake!" Miss Shotsky exclaimed. "And what's this?"

She removed a folded paper that
had been taped to the skeleton's hand.
She read it out loud: "APRIL FOOLS!"
They all burst out laughing.

"Someone has been playing a trick on the whole school!" Mrs. Waters said.

"Well, Mr. Bones is going back where he belongs," Miss Shotsky said. She lifted the school skeleton off the hook.

"Say bye-bye," she said, waving the skeleton's hand. Then she carried it into her office.

Mrs. Waters went to her desk. She looked at her calendar. "Today *is* April Fools' Day," she said. "It totally slipped my mind."

She carried her coat to the closet. She placed it on the hook, then bent down and picked something up off the closet floor. When she turned around, she was holding a pair of sneakers. She turned them over so everyone could see the bottoms.

"Zigzag treads!" Josh said.

"Are *those* the sneakers that everyone's been talking about?" Mr. Dillon said. "How did they get in your coat closet, Mrs. Waters?"

Mrs. Waters stared at her boss for a moment, then shook her head. "I have no idea, Mr. Dillon."

"Um, excuse me, I think I know," Dink said.

Mr. Dillon looked at Dink. The lights glinted off his eyeglasses. "You do? Tell us, Dink."

Dink blushed. "Well, someone decided to play an April Fools' Day joke on the whole school. So he took Miss Shotsky's skeleton and hid it in Mrs. Waters's closet."

Dink looked at Mrs. Waters. "He took your key so you wouldn't be able to open the door."

"But why would this person hide his sneakers?" Mr. Dillon asked.

"Because he left a footprint," Josh

said. "And he planned to make more footprints later."

"And he borrowed Mrs. Waters's powder to do it with," Ruth Rose said, grinning at Dink and Josh.

"He took the key somewhere and had six copies made," Dink went on. "He drew six skeletons and left them and the keys in six different lockers, one for each classroom."

Mr. Dillon shook his head. "Amazing! Why would he do such a thing?"

"I think he wanted all the kids to search for the skeleton," Dink said.

"I'm confused," Mr. Dillon said. He sat in Mrs. Waters's chair. "How could some stranger come into the school and do all this without being seen?"

Dink glanced at Josh and Ruth Rose. They both nodded.

"We think it was someone who works here, sir," Dink said.

"One of the teachers?" Mr. Dillon said. "But who? And *why*?"

Dink, Josh, and Ruth Rose looked at Mr. Dillon. They kept staring until the principal blushed.

"Oh my goodness!" Mrs. Waters cried. "It was you, wasn't it?"

"Caught," Mr. Dillon said, grinning.

"But you wanted to get caught," Ruth Rose said. "That's why you left footprints and keys and notes."

Mr. Dillon nodded. "Yes, I wanted to get caught. You see, I love April Fools' Day. When I was your age, I couldn't wait for this day. I played pranks all the time!"

"I did, too!" Mrs. Waters said. "My sister was always finding frogs in her sweater drawer."

"No one plays tricks or pranks anymore," Mr. Dillon went on. "Each year April first just slips by, unnoticed.

"So I decided that this year would be different. This year, everyone would remember April Fools' Day."

Mr. Dillon kicked off his loafers and pulled on the zigzag sneakers. "I've missed these," he said. "I wear them to school every morning, then change to my loafers."

Dink laughed. "We went around measuring teachers' feet, and all the time those sneakers were in the closet."

The principal grinned. "I have to admit, I had a lot of fun. On Monday I went in to wash my hands at Miss Shotsky's sink. It was early; no one was here. Then I saw the skeleton with her scarf draped around its shoulders, and that's when I got the idea."

His eyes twinkled. "I grabbed the skeleton, came back through our connecting door, and hid it in Mrs. Waters's closet. She leaves the key in the lock, so I just locked the door and kept the key."

"Then you changed your shoes, right?" Josh asked.

Mr. Dillon nodded. "I didn't realize I'd left a footprint. But when you told me that later, I decided to leave more footprints, and that's when I borrowed Mrs. Waters's powder."

"And I expect it back, please," she said.

Everyone laughed again.

Mr. Dillon smiled. "Since you three kids were the first to find Mr. Bones, you get to make the announcement over the intercom."

"What announcement?" Dink asked.

"Why, about the trip, of course! I've hired buses to take the entire school to the aquarium," Mr. Dillon said.

"Everyone is going?" asked Ruth Rose.

"Everyone searched for Mr. Bones, so everyone gets the prize," said Mr. Dillon.

Suddenly Mr. Bones's head popped through the connecting door.

"Even me?" the skeleton asked.

# HAVE YOU READ ALL THE BOOKS IN THE

## A to Z Mysteries®

### SERIES?

## Help Dink, Josh, and Ruth Rose...

...solve mysteries from A to Z!

Collect clues with
Dink, Josh, and Ruth Rose
in their next exciting
adventure!

# THE
# TALKING
# T. REX

"Thanks for coming, folks!" Jud said to the crowd.

Jud pointed his mike at the dinosaur. "Now I'd like you all to meet my friend Tyrone. Tyrone, why don't you tell these good folks about yourself?" he said.

Nothing happened. Tyrone stood silent and still.

Then, suddenly, Tyrone's tail moved to the right, then to the left. His mouth opened and Tyrone said, "Hi!" in a deep voice.

"HI, TYRONE!" the crowd yelled back.

"How many of you know what kind of dinosaur I am?" Tyrone asked.

Every kid and adult raised a hand. "Tyrannosaurus!"

# A TO Z MYSTERIES® fans, check out Ron Roy's other great mystery series!

# Capital Mysteries

#1: Who Cloned the President?
#2: Kidnapped at the Capital
#3: The Skeleton in the Smithsonian
#4: A Spy in the White House
#5: Who Broke Lincoln's Thumb?
#6: Fireworks at the FBI
#7: Trouble at the Treasury
#8: Mystery at the Washington Monument
#9: A Thief at the National Zoo
#10: The Election-Day Disaster
#11: The Secret at Jefferson's Mansion
#12: The Ghost at Camp David
#13: Trapped on the D.C. Train!
#14: Turkey Trouble on the National Mall

January Joker
February Friend
March Mischief
April Adventure
May Magic
June Jam
July Jitters
August Acrobat
September Sneakers
October Ogre
November Night
December Dog
New Year's Eve Thieves

If you like **A TO Z MYSTERIES**®, take a swing at

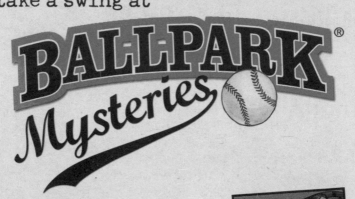

BALLPARK® Mysteries

#1: The Fenway Foul-Up

#2: The Pinstripe Ghost

#3: The L.A. Dodger

#4: The Astro Outlaw

#5: The All-Star Joker

#6: The Wrigley Riddle

#7: The San Francisco Splash

#8: The Missing Marlin

#9: The Philly Fake

#10: The Rookie Blue Jay

#11: The Tiger Troubles